and the Mystic Boots

By Rachel Cladingbowl and Harriet Jones

Illustrations by Charli Vince

Published by Paramecium Press

Paramecium Press Ltd

First published in Great Britain by Paramecium Press Ltd in 2021
Text copyright © Rachel Cladingbowl and Harriet Jones 2021
Illustrations copyright © Charli Vince 2021

A CIP catalogue record for this book is available from the British Library.

IBSN 978-1-8382906-0-3

Printed on 100% recycled paper by Swallowtail Printers, Norwich UK

Foreword by Jess French

Most people don't know that there is a universe of miniature creatures that exists all around us. But after reading this book and adventuring with Aggi and her friends, you will know all about the wonderful protist world, and will even get to know some of these creatures on first name terms!

It is so important that children learn about the tiny creatures that rule the world, and that every living thing, no matter how small, is important.

Chapter One

"It's not fair!"

Aggi had wanted to be a member of the Dinosaur Explorers Club since the day she had hatched. Today she wanted it more than anything. Today was the Jurassic Cup, a contest to discover the smallest living thing.

"You're too young," said Big Ava, gently. "Granny Apatosaurus is coming to look after you."

Aggi hung her head so low it touched the ground.

Even Archibald was going. Her lazy brother didn't even *like* exploring.

"Maybe next year," said Big Ava. "Now, eat your plants."

"I don't want plants," sulked Aggi. "I want crocodiles."

Big Ava looked horrified. Archibald snorted. "We're herbivores," he teased. "Don't you know anything?"

Aggi glared at her brother. It wasn't fair. She just knew she could win the Jurassic Cup, if only she had the chance.

3

Chapter Two

The smallest thing Aggi could find was a wasp. She tried to catch it, but it stung her face and flew away.

"Will you help me discover the smallest living thing?" Aggi asked Granny Apatosaurus.

Granny was old and crumpled and her tummy dragged on the ground when she walked.

Granny Apatosaurus screwed up her eyes. "Who said... Ouch!" Granny Apatosaurus bumped smack bang into a tree. She rubbed her head. "Who put that there? You're so untidy!"

Aggi sighed. Granny Apatosaurus couldn't even see her. She was the most boring Granny ever.

It was going to be a long day.

Unless...

Without looking back, Aggi stomped off through the undergrowth.
She was determined to find the smallest living thing, all by herself.

Chapter Three

As Aggi approached the lake she was
stomping so hard her legs hurt. She
chanted in time with her stomps:

"This world is boring. This world IS
BORING. THIS WORLD IS..."

"Exciting?"

Aggi jumped. She twisted her neck
and saw a dozy Stegosaurus, peering at
her through one half-open eye.

"Did I make you jump?" the Stegosaurus yawned. "You woke me up. Why are you stomping and complaining on such a lovely morning?"

Thinking about feeling cross and sorry for herself made Aggi feel cross and sorry for herself all over again.

"It is *not* a lovely morning," she snapped. "There is nothing to do and nothing to see. All I wanted was to be in the Dinosaur Explorers Club and discover the smallest living thing."

"Hmmm... There is always something to see if you know where to look," disagreed the Stegosaurus. "By the way, I'm Steg."

"I'm Aggi," said Aggi. "And I don't know where to look. All I found was a stupid wasp and it stung me."

9

"Hmmm..." Steg slowly chewed a fern. "I know what you need."

Steg plodded off into the undergrowth. He returned with two tiny objects. They were like little feet without legs.

"What are *they*?" Aggi stared, wide-eyed.

"The Mystic Boots," whispered Steg, mysteriously. "They will take you on an adventure."

Aggi's eyes grew bigger than Steg's head.

"Where did you get them?" she wondered.

"Well," began Steg, "one night a huge, metal bird crashed into the ferns. A funny little two-legged creature climbed out. My wise old grandfather, who went to university, said it was a human from the future. The human disappeared by sunrise, but he left the boots behind. Put them on."

The Mystic Boots didn't seem scary, but Aggi wasn't sure she wanted to have an adventure. She lifted one foot. She put it down again.

"Will they help me discover the smallest living thing?" Aggi asked, excitedly.

"Maybe," winked Steg.

Chapter Four

"Before you go on your adventure, I have something else for you," said Steg.
It was a strange rectangle with circles sticking out. "It was found beside the boots," Steg explained.

Curiously, Aggi touched one of the circles. It made a whirring noise, then a snap.

"Oh!" exclaimed Aggi. "Look, Steg! It's us!"

Sure enough, Steg and Aggi could see their faces in the Rectangle, looking all wonky.

Aggi had never seen her face in anything except the waterhole before.

"How did that happen?" Aggi
laughed. Steg didn't know.
"I didn't grow up with technology,"
he said.
Aggi touched another circle.
"Oh no!" she exclaimed.

Now there was another picture on the Rectangle. It was a small, two-legged creature. Its tiny mouth was wide open in terror and it was hanging in the air with one leg.

"How unfortunate," said Steg, hanging the Rectangle around Aggi's neck. "Now put on the Mystic Boots and enjoy your adventure."

Chapter Five

Aggi felt as though she was falling. Steg faded, then disappeared.

"Ouch!" said a squeaky voice. "You're standing on me!"

Aggi jumped. She stepped aside and immediately started sinking.

She was underwater! Kicking and gasping, Aggi clung to the lump she had been standing on. It had four useful points sticking out of it.

"Well," said the lump, "since you've rudely invaded my space, we might as well chat. I'm Ceratium. And don't squeeze my horn!"

"I'm Aggi," said Aggi, clinging tightly. She was talking and breathing underwater! Had she turned into a fish?

"Can I eat you?" pondered Ceratium. "You might taste nice."

Aggi was horrified. "No! Besides," she added, "I'm a big dinosaur and funny lumps can't eat dinosaurs."

"You look tiny to me," said Ceratium.

Aggi laughed. She was starting to relax.

"I'm an Apatosaurus. We are huge. When I grow up, nothing will eat me."

"Well, I am just about the smallest thing ever," replied Ceratium. "I am smaller than a grain of sand. And you are smaller than me."

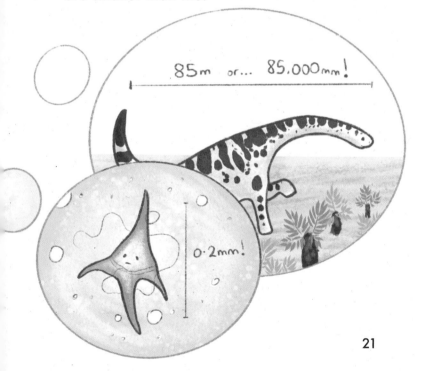

85m or... 85,000mm!

0.2mm!

Aggi thought being smaller than a grain of sand seemed very dangerous.

"What are you?" she wondered, curiously. "Are you a swimming plant?"

"A plant?" retorted Ceratium. "I am not!"

"A fish?" Aggi tried again.

"Wrong!"

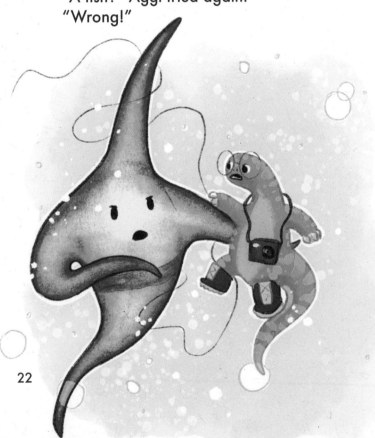

22

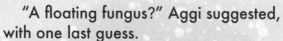

"A floating fungus?" Aggi suggested, with one last guess.

"How would you like to be called a fungus?" snorted Ceratium. **"QUICK! MOVE!"**

Aggi swung her neck around. An enormous mouth was zooming towards them. It looked like a big, black hole.

23

"I can't swim!" Aggi panicked. "Help!
What's that?!"

"A fish," said Ceratium. "And you'd
better learn quickly!"

Aggi froze. Ceratium sighed. "Such a
time waster! I *suppose* you can swim
with me. Then I can eat you — if we
survive."

Aggi shuddered. Suddenly she wished she had stayed with Granny Apatosaurus. Perhaps Granny wasn't so boring after all.

Together, they swam in a zigzag pattern. But the Mouth was getting closer. And closer. And closer.

"Hurry!" pleaded Aggi. "Why are we going all over the place?"

"It's the way I twist," said Ceratium. "Sorry."

Aggi thought of Big Ava arriving home, ready to wrap her up in a big neck hug.

She thought of Archibald, who was annoying but sometimes funny. She even thought of her father, Alfonso the Amazing, who she hadn't seen since the terrible night of the volcano.

"How can you be so calm?" Aggi cried. "We're about to be eaten!"

"It happens all the time round here!" replied Ceratium.

The Mouth zoomed along, swallowing everything in its path. Aggi closed her eyes and prepared for the worst.

Chapter Six

The Mouth sped past, tossing them about like bits of old weed.

"That was close!" Aggi breathed a sigh of relief. "It didn't see us."

"Of course not," scoffed Ceratium. "We're too small."

"You still haven't told me what you are," remembered Aggi. "I told you I'm an Apatosaurus. Usually we are too big to be eaten. Archibald says we dinosaurs rule the world."

"Big. Small. We all rely on each other," said Ceratium, wisely. "We all have jobs to do. The world belongs to no one. I'm a protist."

"What are you protesting about?" asked Aggi.

"Protist, not protest. Clean your ears out. But if I *was* protesting, it would be about *you* disturbing my peace."

"What *is* a protist?" wondered Aggi.

"A protist is made up of just one cell," explained Ceratium. "Imagine your body is like a rock pool full of sand. All the grains of sand work together to make your body the way it is. You are all the grains of sand in the rock pool — trillions of them. My body is just like one of the grains of sand."

"Wow," said Aggi.

"I am only one cell," continued Ceratium, "yet I breathe and eat just like you. And I can swim."

Aggi thought for a moment. "So, what do I have that you don't?"

"You have a brain."

Aggi tried to imagine not having a brain.

31

They floated along in silence. A jellyfish danced by. As they headed upwards, sunlight filtered through.

"I'm hungry," announced Ceratium. "It's lunchtime. Would you care to join me? I don't want to eat you yet. I might be allergic."

Aggi's tummy felt like an empty hole. She wondered what lunch would be. Anything but plants!

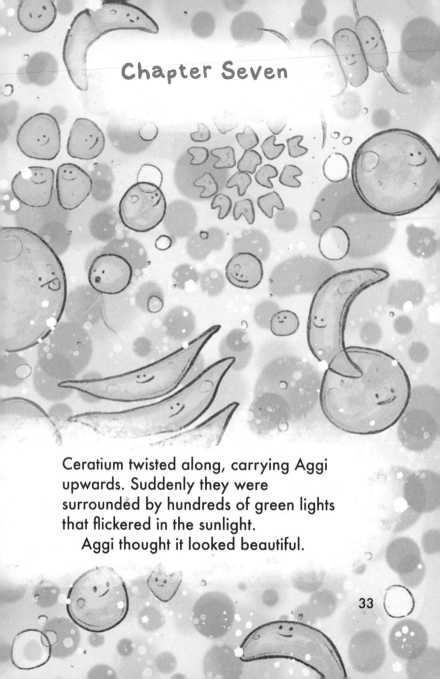

Chapter Seven

Ceratium twisted along, carrying Aggi
upwards. Suddenly they were
surrounded by hundreds of green lights
that flickered in the sunlight.

Aggi thought it looked beautiful.

Suddenly Aggi remembered the Rectangle. It was still hanging around her neck.

She showed Ceratium the circles, and the picture with Steg appeared.

34

One of Ceratium's horns knocked the Rectangle. Just like before, it whirred and snapped. A big picture of Ceratium appeared, with Aggi in the background.

"How did that happen?" Ceratium wanted to know.

"No idea," shrugged Aggi.

"Ha ha hee hee!"

"What was that?" Aggi couldn't see anything except the green lights.

"We're here! We're here!"

"Where?" Aggi wondered, aloud.

"Thecirclesmakethepicturesthecircles makethepictures!"

"You two are silly!"

"Sillysillysillysilly!"

"My name is Alga!"

"So is mine!"

"I'm Alga too!"

"We're all called Alga!"

"Alga, Alga, Alga!"

"How confusing!" laughed Aggi, as a peal of tuneful giggling broke out. "But I still can't see you!" She craned her neck as they floated through the flickering green.

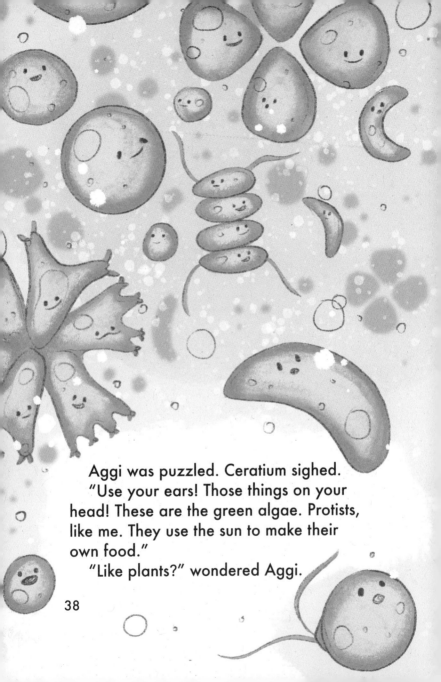

Aggi was puzzled. Ceratium sighed.
"Use your ears! Those things on your
head! These are the green algae. Protists,
like me. They use the sun to make their
own food."

"Like plants?" wondered Aggi.

38

"Exactly," said Ceratium. "And they are telling us that The Circles Make the Pictures."

Aggi blinked. Of course! Thecirclesmakethepictures!

Aggi and Ceratium spent ten lovely minutes making pictures with the Rectangle. Aggi pressed the circles. Ceratium had an eye for the perfect setting.

"Over here," Ceratium said. "The light is perfect. Look, there's an amoeba."

"You can see through him!" Aggi exclaimed. "And he is changing shape!"

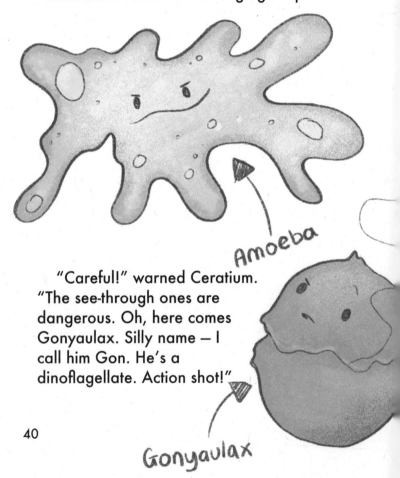

Amoeba

"Careful!" warned Ceratium. "The see-through ones are dangerous. Oh, here comes Gonyaulax. Silly name — I call him Gon. He's a dinoflagellate. Action shot!"

Gonyaulax

40

"Is a dinoflagellate a dinosaur like me?" wondered Aggi.

"No," replied Ceratium. "It's a protist, like me. In fact, I am a type of dinoflagellate myself."

They carried on taking pictures until they were too hungry to think of anything except lunch.

"What *is* for lunch?" Aggi asked.

"It's right here." Ceratium twisted towards the algae, who started squealing.

"Helphelphelphelp!"

Aggi was horrified.

"No! You can't eat *them*!" she cried. "They helped us!"

41

"It's how it works." Ceratium moved forwards as Alga, Alga and every other Alga shrank backwards. "Some protists eat other protists."

"Oh, but... please don't!" Aggi couldn't bear to see the beautiful Algas all gobbled up.

"We won't eat them all," promised Ceratium.

Aggi tried to hang back but she was pulled along by Ceratium. "No, I can't."

"I've no time for fussy eaters," tutted Ceratium. "Next time bring a packed lunch."

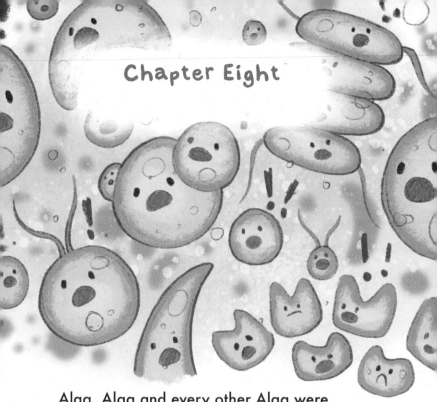

Chapter Eight

Alga, Alga and every other Alga were shaking in terror.

"Nonononononononono!"

"Please stop!" protested Aggi.

But Ceratium twisted along, hungrily. Suddenly a whole gang of protists just like Ceratium appeared and joined in.

The water was like a churned up battleground.

All the Algas squealed in fright. Aggi closed her eyes and counted to ten. When she opened them she thought Alga, Alga and every other Alga would be gone.

Instead, Ceratium's friends had vanished, the algae were as still as statues, and she was face to face with a Very Hairy Monster.

And it was see-through!
"AAAAAAAGGGGGGGHHHH!!"
screamed Aggi.

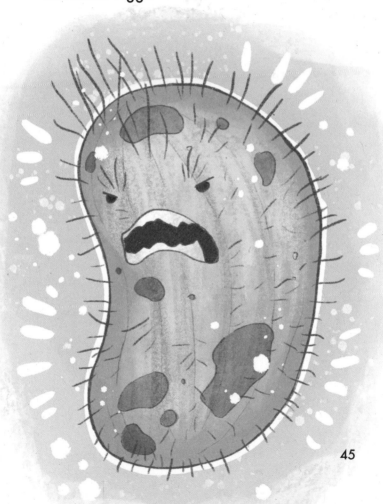

"YUM YUM!" said the Very Hairy Monster, excitedly. "Something new and tasty looking! I haven't eaten for ten minutes and twenty-four seconds."

"Lucky you," muttered Ceratium.

Aggi couldn't believe Ceratium was still thinking about lunch.

"We're about to be eaten!" she cried. "Do something!"

"It's you she wants to eat," said Ceratium. "Cilla loves new flavours. And she's a very fast swimmer. She won free-style in the Protist Olympics. You are doomed."

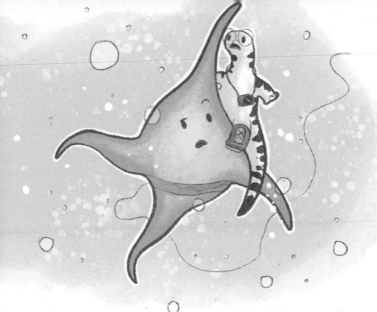

The Very Hairy Monster opened its very hairy mouth. Aggi screamed again. Why had she put on those stupid boots?

Suddenly she missed Granny Apatosaurus, Big Ava and annoying Archibald more than anything in the world.

She imagined her father, Alfonso the Amazing, strong and proud before the volcano erupted and took him away. She missed him so much.

Above all, she wished this nightmare would end and she would wake up at home.

Chapter Nine

At the very last second, Gon appeared and whisked Aggi to safety. Defeated, the Very Hairy Monster skulked off in a very bad mood.

"She's always grumpy," said Ceratium. "Wouldn't you be if you had that hairstyle? It went out with the Triassic."

Ceratium thanked Gon for saving Aggi and they arranged to meet for a catch-up on Thursday.

"That was Cilla Cilia," explained Ceratium.

"Sillier than who?" spluttered Aggi. All this twisting was making her travel sick.

"No, Cilla Cilia, the Ciliate."

"Is that a tongue twister?" frowned Aggi.

"If you can say Cilla Cilia Ciliate ten times I promise not to eat you. I'm even starting to like you."

Aggi managed to say Cilla Cilia Ciliate three times. Ceratium managed four times.

"Let's make it more challenging," suggested Ceratium. "Now you have to say Silly Cilla Cilia Ciliate as many times as you can."

That was impossible for them both.

cilla cilla...

silly cilla...

49

Chapter Ten

Aggi's energy was fading.

"I'm going to be sick from hunger," she complained. "Aren't you?"

"I have topped up my energy using sunlight," declared Ceratium. "But let's visit Flagella Awesome. She cooks the most amazing bacteria dishes. Your taste buds will drool!"

"Who is Flagella Awesome?" Aggi thought bacteria might make a nice change from plants. She hoped it wasn't spicy.

"Who is Flagella Awesome? Only the most famous protist chef ever!" exclaimed Ceratium. "Haven't you seen Aqua Chef?"

Aggi hadn't.

Dreaming of food, they twisted along together. To pass the time, Aggi told Ceratium about how unfair it was that she couldn't join the Dinosaur Explorers Club.

"You're already an explorer," Ceratium told her. "You don't need to be in a club."

Flagella Awesome and her staff were cooking up a storm. There were bacteria everywhere. It smelled delicious.

"Afternoon! I'm throwing a party!" Flagella told them. "You're both invited."

52

Flagella Awesome had two flagella and an extra arm, which was useful for multitasking. But so many guests arrived they had trouble serving up all the bacteria. Ceratium and Aggi offered to help. Between them, they could carry five dishes at once. Ceratium kept stealing the spirally bacteria.

"They're my favourites," Ceratium explained.

53

"Would you two like a job?" Flagella Awesome asked, when all the dishes were served. "I'm short-staffed."

Aggi thanked Flagella, but said she wasn't local.

Ceratium thought it was too much of a commitment.

Ceratium and Aggi stayed at the party for hours. The bacteria were delicious.

Cilla Cilia had done her hair up in a new style and was perfectly behaved.

They all danced in the water, showing off their moves in the light made by Gon and his friends, who glowed in the dark.

55

Ceratium was brilliant at the Twist. Nobody tried to eat Alga, Alga, or any other Alga.

Aggi showed Flagella Awesome the Rectangle. They made a picture together. Flagella signed the Rectangle in squid ink.

"The squid died from natural causes," Flagella assured her. "It collided with a starfish. I ordered the ink from Saltwater Solutions, delivered by Dragonfly."

As they danced, Aggi wondered how such an amazing world could have existed without her even knowing. Steg was right — this world wasn't boring at all. She had discovered so many fascinating creatures. Perhaps she was the best dinosaur explorer to have ever lived.

Aggi was having so much fun she danced her boots off.

57

Chapter Eleven

"Aha, you're back."

Steg slowly opened one eye. Aggi looked across the undergrowth. The trees were the same. The rocks were the same. Even the lake was the same. It looked dull and empty.

"Did you enjoy your adventure?" Steg wanted to know. "And where are my boots? Don't tell me you've lost them?"

Aggi glanced down at her bare feet.
"Sorry," she said.

"Never mind," said Steg. "I'm not the
adventurous sort anyway."

Chapter Twelve

Big Ava and Archibald were untangling
Granny Apatosaurus. Her tail was wound
round a tree and her head was stuck
between two rocks.

"I told you to tidy those trees up!"
complained Granny Apatosaurus.

"Where have you been, Aggi?" asked
Big Ava.

"I had the best day ever!" grinned
Aggi. "Did you win the Jurassic Cup?"

Big Ava sighed as Granny Apatosaurus wriggled and moaned.

"We came two-hundred-and-sixty-fourth."

"It wasn't fair!" whined Archibald. "Dan Dryosaurus stole our ant and came third. Never trust anyone with a beak!"

"I know of something much smaller than an ant," Aggi declared. "Have you heard of a protist?"

"That's not a real thing," snorted Archibald, as he went off to lie around doing nothing.

Aggi plodded off happily.

That night, Aggi looked at all her pictures — Steg, Ceratium, all the Algas, Gon, Flagella Awesome and even Cilla Cilia and her new hair.

Then she buried the Rectangle in the earth so that Archibald couldn't steal it and closed her eyes contentedly.

As she slept, Aggi dreamed. She was by the waterhole when a shadow crept up behind her.

As she turned, she saw Alfonso the Amazing, lit up by the sun.

"You are the best dinosaur explorer ever," said Alfonso the Amazing, smiling. "And I am the proudest father to have ever lived."

65

The End

Let me introduce you to some of my friends!

We all live together in the lake.

My great friend Cilla Ciliate (Sill-ee-ate)

You may be wondering how big Cilla Ciliate is? Well, you could fit about four of her on one full stop – imagine that! Cilla Ciliate eats very small creatures like bacteria. You could fit hundreds of bacteria on one full stop! Why is she called a ciliate, you might ask? It is because of all the hairs she is covered with. They are called cilia, and she beats them like little paddles so she can swim around. And she can swim really fast!

Flagella Awesome (fla-jell ah)

Flagella Awesome is quite a bit smaller than me. She swims using the long hair-like things which she beats – they pull her along. I have two of them too. She loves eating bacteria. But if she can't find enough to eat she can also use the sunlight to make food, just like me.

Bacteria (bac-TIR-ree a)

Bacteria are very tasty! They are also tiny, so I need to eat a lot of them. They come in lots of shapes and sizes and are very different creatures to us protists. Bacteria seem to get everywhere and many of them eat the food that spills out from the algae.

69

Gonyaulax (gon-EE O-lax)

Gon is a dinoflagellate, like me, but from a different family of dinoflagellates. He doesn't have the horn-like things that I do. When he gets together with his friends, in huge numbers, they can make the lake look red. And in the dark he can glow and light up the water.

Algae (al-GEE)

I love the algae. Not only are they very tasty but they are beautiful too. They are a lovely rich green colour and they love the sunlight. The algae live near the surface of our lake and use the sunlight to make their food. They are a bit sloppy in their feeding and spill out a lot of their food.

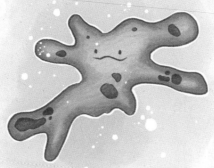

Amoeba (a ME-ba)

When Aggi came to visit we saw an amoeba. Amoebas are so clever. Imagine being able to move everything that is inside you, anywhere in your body and instead of having fixed arms and legs you could just push one out when you wanted to. Everything that is inside them flows through them, pushing against their skin-like coat. This coat then pushes out to form what they call false feet. This is how an amoeba moves around and swallows up its food. I'm very careful around big amoebas because they could eat me. A big one can be about the size of a full stop, perhaps even a little bigger.

You will find me and my friends wherever there is water – in lakes and rivers, in oceans, in the soil. Some friends of mine live in tree holes where they have their own little pool of water.

There are friends of Gon who light up the breaking waves on a beach at night. And friends of Flagella Awesome can gather in huge numbers called a bloom. Some of these blooms are so big they can be seen from space!

Friends of the algae can even live on snow where they turn glaciers pink. Why pink? Well just like you, we protists can get hurt by sunlight and need sun cream too. So, because they are not down in the water but on the surface of the snow, these creatures have pink sun cream!

Some of my friends can carry a nasty poison. When they get eaten by shellfish, they make the shellfish poisonous. Perhaps they shouldn't eat so many of us in one go! Some of our friends live inside animals and plants where there is water. They can make them very sick. There is one illness called malaria. Plasmodium is the protist that causes this, living in the blood of animals. There is one very pretty protist with four pairs of flagella, called Giardia. It lives in the tummy of animals and makes their poo smell disgusting!

We really do live everywhere, but we are so small you can only see the results of what we do, without knowing we are there at all.

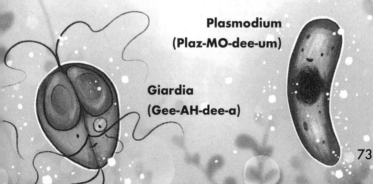

**Plasmodium
(Plaz-MO-dee-um)**

**Giardia
(Gee-AH-dee-a)**

Glossary of some other words and names

Some of the words can be difficult to say. When letters are written in capitals, it means you really have to emphasise them to make the word sound right.

Apatosaurus (a-PAT-o sor-us)
A plant eating dinosaur from the Jurassic times.

Ceratium (sir-RATE EE-um)
A dinoflagellate and a main character of this book!

Cilia (SIL -ee-ah)
Tiny little hair-like structures. They are actually very short flagella. They are used by ciliates to help them swim by beating rows of cilia over their cell surface.

Dinoflagellate (DY-NO fla-jell-ate)
A type of protist. Dinoflagellates have two flagella and some are covered in an armour of scales. They can be a reddish brown colour which comes from the way they use sunlight to make their food.

Dryosarus (DRY-o-saw-us)
   A fast running, plant-eating dinosaur with a beak.

Flagella (fla-jell ah)
   Whip-like structures which some protists have which help them do things like swim and gather food.

Herbivores (HER-be-vorz)
   The name that is given to animals that only eat plants.

Jurassic (jer-RASS-ic)
   A time long ago when dinosaurs roamed the Earth, around 200 million years ago.

Protist (PRO-tist)
   A creature which is made up of just one cell. They eat, breathe, move and create more protists, and they do all this as only a single cell.

Stegosaurus (STEG-o sor-us)
   A dinosaur from the Jurassic with plates along the back.

Reviews for
Aggi and the Mystic Boots

"A unique and entertaining dive into the watery world of microbes." - Dr Alan Warren, Protistologist, Natural History Museum, past president of Protistology UK.

"The world's smallest safari adventure with some of nature's coolest characters." - Professor Ben Garrod, biologist and presenter.

"My grandchildren really loved this story, and the illustrations, and I was happy to see mixotrophs in there!" - Dr Dale Holen, Aquatic Ecologist and Associate Professor of Biology, Penn State University.

"It is brilliant. Really sciency and fun and I learned a lot." - Ezra May (age 7)

"I thought the book was fantastic."
- Robyn Powley (age 5)

"I love this dinosaur adventure." - Aaron Manning (age 9)